D1692690

ETERNAL AUTUMN
Poetry Collection

CAYTE CUTRO

GLASSSPIDERPUBLISHING

Cover design by Judith S. Design & Creativity
www.judithsdesign.com
Published by Glass Spider Publishing
www.glassspiderpublishing.com

I dedicate this book to the many people who have inspired my poetry—by loving me, hurting me, hating me, or saving me.

Contents

SUMMER

AUTUMN

Prologue

One day, I will feel at peace; either because I will have everything that I have ever wanted, or because I will have accepted that I never will.

SPRING

Our Deal

Relying on my intuition
With my agony abating
Betting all my everything
Knowing you were waiting

This deal we've made
Amid all of life's commotions
Before ever an encounter
Before igniting our emotions

Quick sparks, then slow burns
So unexpectedly alluring
Exceptionally amusing
Yet, euphoric and enduring

This deal we've made
To trust in this possibility
Lessons learned in patience
Lessons learned in durability

Mixing and merging patterns
Tightening all our quirks and screws
Decorating each other's lives
With shades of yellows, greens, and blues

This deal we've made
This delicate dichotomy
All that you have borrowed
All that you have brought to me

Translating and deciphering
All our simplified complexity
Marveling at the perfectness
Of our magical perplexity

This deal we've made
Betting against this world's objection
With your measured approach to loving me
With my impulsive, raw affection

In the Nick of Time

In the nick of time
You saved my smile
Safe in my sadness
Limp from my loneliness

Without words
You won over my worries
My waning hope
And turned them into wonder

In the nick of time
You figured out my faults
But did not try to fix them
Forgiving my foolish fantasies

How did you know
That the person I promised
Not the person I pretended
Was there all along?

In the nick of time
You opened your heart to me
Your arms to me, your life to me
And awoke my weary heart
In the nick of time

A Fragile Path

Dare you start the path to my heart?
Please know—it begins at my hand
Your pitied past I'll tear apart
Your dooming doubt be damned

Ever in shame you'll deny my name?
Will your conscience take a fall?
My frozen soul will bear the blame
But in time, I'll forgive it all

Have you yet met the word "regret?"
Your eyes tell me to stay
To borrow my heart, you'll fall in debt
Closing the door when you pray

Angelic eyes could be clouds in disguise
Will they rain the day that I'm lost?
My faith in love won't meet such demise
So, search for me—whatever the cost

Will our senses cease to dwell in peace?
Will our hands unlock from grasp?
Minds at ease—love is bound to increase
But I'll let go, if ever you'd ask

An altered fate, not early, nor late
As twilight veils my smile
A fragile path to me, your "Kate"
Enduring this love for a while

Endearing Love

I was succumbing to comfort
Your cue to appear
With your caramel kindness
And chocolaty cheer

A little too late
Yet right on time
As I was setting my ways
And watching my dime

Investing my heart,
My time, my space
As I barter my pride
You exchange your embrace

Conventionally content
Your palm presses mine
In subconscious affection
Our legs intertwine

I want to want this
Whatever "this" may be
With your misplaced attention
And my stubborn decree

Enduring my doubt
Through all four seasons
An endearing love
For uncertain reasons

So here is my heart,
My time, my space
It is your turn to barter
I am well worth the chase

Now

Now…
With your gold intentions and red desire
Never mind your blue emotion

Now…
Before you search my attic
You open my cellar door

Now…
Your smile attains my trust
While my smile sparks your lust

Now…
With clever kisses and roaming fingers
Break right through the silence that lingers

Now…
You tease my laugh and my dimly lit wit
Exchange with me your scent and your spit

Now…
You jerk my tears, I jerk your string
What happens in fall to our feelings of spring?

Now…
Is that a knife behind your back?
I'll take the chance, but faith, I lack

Now…
You open my mind to the dreams I store
You keep the soul that I adore

Now…
In the dark
Your starry eyes
And moon above me
In the end
You may even love me
But for Now…
We will wait for later

Our Evening Hour

Anxiously waiting
Your ten o'clock Titos text
My day is complete

Burning For You

The minutes meander
My feet in a pace
Wistfully longing
To leap into embrace

Your "come hither" gaze
The chills through my spine
The zesty elation
When your eyes lock with mine

Bashful, yet bold
We traipse to the next floor
Slip out of your costume
Behind my closed door

Carouse and arouse me
Unravel my riddle
Your frisky phalanges
Play my parts like a fiddle

Sparking and sizzling
A flame flaring blue
Extinguish these embers
While I'm burning for you

Your titillating tongue
Mixed with fervent affection
The euphoric concoction
From your lustful injection

Breathless and bruised
All feverish and fizzy
Our tumultuous tryst
Leaves my mind in a tizzy

Our impassioned encounter
Tattooed into my head
Your enslaving essence
Infused into my bed

Eternally Mine

With my shaky hand
You are alive on paper
Eternally mine

The Flame

The flame is lit
The spell is cast
We wait and sit
As an hour passed

Could this be fate?
Again, we meet
I hesitate
But crave the heat

Your touch, a glance
So risky, so wrong
I'll take this chance
And stare too long

My name—a stain
On your feeble brain
Your lips—like prints
On my fingertips

Is this my shame?
I lost my will
Am I to blame
For wanting you still?

Let's say goodbye
Until fate says when
I'll bide my time
Until we meet again

The fault is mine
Bleeding with blame
Shielding your shrine
Still holding the flame

Compass

The moon guides my path
Perpetual, enduring
My compass to you

Spring Fling

A conspiring glare
The springtime in my hair
Lure me into your leisured lair

To borrow now, or later, to keep?
The reach to my soul
Is much too steep

You split my thighs
With your snow-white lies
But is this yours, or my demise?

Ripping a hole
In my patchwork soul
Validating voids and gaining our goal

Pillows drenched with our signature scent
A memento of the romp we spent
Is today's bliss tomorrow's repent?

The hour passed, the deed is done
And in the end, our whim was won
Goodbye, my friend—This sure was fun

Fate

Without a compass
Or sense of direction
I wandered my way
To your eager affection

Some say it is "fate"
Or just "meant to be"
It was written in stars
Or a fateful decree

But what if I stumbled
Or stopped for some sleep
Could I have altered this fate
Denying my keep?

Whatever the outcome
If plans were derailed
I trust that our fate
Would have somehow prevailed

Your Ink

Injecting your ink
So deeply inside of me
To spill out my pen

Surrender

Love is a war
In which all fools partake
But I'm not a fool
With my heart set to break

In attempt for my truth
They send asks of *"why?"*
No love shall I release them
Their questions lack reply

Soldiers amidst the battle
In the war to win my heart
They stab me with their wooden swords
That splinter and split apart

To dig in deep
They set their goal
To claim my love,
My heart, my soul

I won't be captured
Or be a casualty of
Their quests for all
My sour love

The one in red
Who dropped his sword
Then bared his flag
My heart adored

In his eyes afire
My emotions scold
In his ardent arms
My defenses unfold

Dropping my will
My soul defender
So, for him, my love
I will surrender

Inferno

If merely looking at you
Ignites a five-foot flame in my soul
Just imagine
The inferno that would blaze
If ever I touch you

Mincing Words

"You're mincing words again,"
He'll often say
Well, of course I am
That's a poet's way

A smidgen of truth
A sprinkling of time
Weaving in rhythm
Then dusting with rhyme

Bewildered and Bemused

Your mind, bewildered
My soul, unfiltered

Your tongue, serrated
My body, berated

Your phallus, inflated
My posy, elated

Our bodies, infused
My conscience, bemused

Wrap Forever in "I Do"

Entwined in love
They stand before
The golden path
With the silver door

In anxious strides
They stagger no more
Engulfed in light
Before the lord

For this is love
And so, some weep
They free the doves
They could not keep

All faults and fears
They put to sleep
They pass the step
That once looked steep

For in her hand
He places spring
Enduring all
The winters bring

For on her hand
He'll place a ring
A promise of love
And everything

For this is love
And this is true
With something borrowed
Something blue

An old emotion
A marriage new
They wrap forever
In "I do"

Sweet Talker

Your syrupy gibberish
I would firmly resist
Has become an addiction
I now eagerly insist

The Boy on the Raft

You have always been
And will forever be
The boy on the raft
In the frothy Jersey sea

Strategically stinging me
With sporadic splashes
Saltwater pooling
On your lengthy lashes

Riding the mid-day waves
Coyly conveying "no fear"
All too conveniently
Your raft floating near

Striking up a conversation
With *"Do you live near here?"*
Tongue-tied, I stammered *"Yes"*
You said *"We're renting near the pier"*

Why were you even talking to me?
An older boy, so confident, so cute
Me—awkwardly developing
In my hand-me-down swimsuit

Not to Andrea—her long, straight hair
With its golden Sun-In sheen
Nor Erin, with her too-cute dimples
Her legs—annoyingly lean

You asked me about my age
I rounded up—just a tad
You remarked that I looked older
That the difference was not so bad

You said that you'd return here
On the dunes, between seven and eight
And said that I should meet you
That you would stay right there and wait

I agreed with a smile, in six shades of red
Nervous, confused, but mostly giddy
Thinking of all the artful effort
To make myself look pretty

Using my sister's makeup
In her loose-fitting shirt and pants
I vaguely saw my beauty
In the mirror, at just a glance

With my friends' avid encouragement
I traipsed towards where you would be
With ten more steps to meet you
I turned around to flee

I was not yet ready to meet you then
To feel the force of fate
A lifetime of regret and wondering
How long the boy on the raft would wait

One Minute of Time

One minute of time alone with you
Fuels my lonesome soul for days

One light touch of your hand
Soothes my restless mind

One bashful, yet bold, kiss on my lips
Awakens my languished spirit

One deep breath of you
Resuscitates my withering heart

I ask for so little of you…
Just one minute of time

True Beauty

Looking through your amber eyes
Familiar and warm they glow
If I stare a little longer
Such beauty they will show

Yet as I trust in your wood-like eyes
And find them as secure
I tend to follow eyes that glimmer
A deep, or soft, azure

Neither with trust nor security do I stare
But only to marvel
In such boundless beauty
Gleaming blue eyes glare

Falling again into deep blue pools
Which seem to cast a curse
I find comfort in your brown eyes
Whenever blue eyes grow perverse

Naïve and raw
I've followed blue eyes in awe
Your brown eyes have a deeper beauty
Far deeper than what I often saw

My Happy Place

Soothing squawks, in flocks
Sifting sand through shriveled hands
Basking in kismet

SUMMER

Heads, or Tails?

Teetering between
The "what she *should…*"
Versus
The "what she *could…*"

Begging
For my advice
But then, instantly
Thinking twice

Choosing the pleasant poison
Over the putrid elixir
Well aware, that the former may kill her
While the latter may fix her

Into the air
The coin flickers and flails
Calling out *"heads"*
Yet praying for tails

In the end, as you know
There was nothing to decide
Her heart is what leads her
While her head must abide

Selfless

Dandelion gold
Beckoning to be cherished
Ravaged for your wish

Stinger

Flouncing from flower to flower
Lured by their vibrant visage
Their plush petals
Or provocative perfume

Injecting your stinger
Calculating each contact
Rotating and returning
In your quest for the sweetest nectar

Pavonine Eyes

Pavonine eyes
That stone-still stare
Clashing with skies
In angelic flair

Lynching love
From my vulnerable heart
As dear as doves
Then, as dire as darts

Piercing my mind
Like a cold steal dagger
No scars will you find
Not a stain, nor a stagger

Luring with lies
No resistance to believe
Hell in disguise
Only misery to receive

Possessing such power
As many depict them
Eyes that won't cower
For I'm their last victim

Black Cherry

I drink in excess
In the notes of black cherry
You come back to me

Settled

Just because something isn't right
Doesn't make it wrong
Just as one bad verse
Won't ruin a song

So, I've settled for you
Exchanging my musts for my mights
To avoid being "out there"
To evade lonesome nights

So, we'll "dinner and a movie"
With our half-faked affection
To be someone's "someone"
And yield my cat collection

The Reset Button

Frantically fumbling
For the button to reset
Back one minute in time
Before my words
And your ears
Abruptly met

One More Hour

Sun scorching my skin
Breezes blowing soothingly
Just one more hour

My Gifts

I planted plum-purple pansies
In your garish garden
You let the waxy weeds
Weave through them

I baked you my prized pastries
And caramel covered confections
You spit them out
Proclaiming them "too sweet"

I coerced you into the consoling sunlight
You squinted and squirmed
Then scurried away
To your secluded cave

I enveloped you in my amorous arms
Covered you with kisses
You pulled away from me
To lurk and loll alone

With my pride intact
I have one last gracious gift to give you,
My darling,
The gift of "Goodbye"

Eager Daggers

Calculating your attack
Will it be eight pats, or perhaps ten?
Your eager daggers haunt me

Your Toy

Wind me up
To gain hours of amusement

Pull my cord
To hear me praise you

Flip my switch
To light up your darkness

Take me to your bed
To dispel your loneliness

Plug me in
To recharge my power

Press my reset button
To restore my settings

Place me on a shelf with the others
To punish me when I bore you

Dust me off
To lend me out

Dismantle me
To reassemble me

Shove me in a closet
Kick me under the bed

Discard me
When my parts look worn

Ultimately, replace me
With something new

I Carry Your Memories

You share with me
So many of your memories
Hastily handing them over to me
One by one

Constructing the simple, yet complex
Story of "you"
Not skipping over
Any of the unpleasant parts

I am an empathetic listener
A captive audience of one
Flattered you trust me
With such intimate moments

Snapshots of your boyhood fashions
Photos of your family trips
Scribblings of your inner thoughts
Secrets and insecurities

I grow to love you at age 8…16…23
And all ages in-between
As if I had always known you
As if I had always loved you

I listen attentively, and curiously
Even to the repeats
I could probably retell your stories
Word-for-word

Yet, despite your eagerness
To share your memories
You won't give me a basket
To hold them all

They are weighing so heavily in my arms
And in my heart
And I'm unsure of
What you want me to do with them all

I don't dare tell you of the pain
Your memories are causing me
In fear that you'll stop sharing
And I'll stop learning

So, I carry your memories
With only one clear purpose
To feel the pain of loving
Only the story of you

Irrational

Irrational? No!
Emotional…Romantic!
You callous robot

Green Light

Yielding at a yellow light
That slowly turns red
All the while, time escapes
He stares in admiration

He anxiously waits for a green light
Rehearsing his pitch
A moment in silence
Turns into eternity

He becomes distracted
Blinking his strained eyes
Sabotaged by subconsciousness
Or obstructed by fear

Now sitting at a red light
Again...or still?
Knowing another green light will not come
For another eternity...if ever

He never spoke a word to her
Never extended a hand, less his heart
Yielding at a yellow light
Too much time escaped

Locked Door

What dwells beyond your locked door?
You crack it open for mere moments
Will you ever let me in?

I Search For You

I search for you in silence
Where worthless words will sleep
Despite the still tranquility
I never hear a peep

I search for you in chaos
Through the cackles in the crowd
And although I join the madness
You never are avowed

I search for you in darkness
Trusting my hands to find your face
Frightfully I flounder
I never feel a trace

I search for you at sunrise
When the atmosphere is clear
While hopeful and determined
You never do appear

All the while I search for you
So longingly and foolishly
I never stop to wonder
Do you ever search for me?

UNO!

Red rage, blue sorrow
Joyful yellow, serene green
Your moods, like UNO!

The Elephant

Let's give the elephant
A proper name
After all, it appears
He has been with us this whole time

Discerning our thoughts
Watching our inactions
Hoping we wouldn't find our courage
Or else, he would be annihilated

Then, we would be left here
To clean up all the mess
He would leave behind
Or more likely, run away from it all

Go or Stay?

The difference
Between "go" and "stay"
Face the agony now
Or let the torture delay

Memory Lane

I took a stroll down our memory lane
The grass was unruly and unkept

Weeds were woven through the rails
Rocks were sharp and overturned

Bitter wind wafted through the elms
Scents of sadness from decaying leaves

Robins warbled in a nervous pitch
A dense fog blurred the pathway before me

We used to stroll together, hand-in-hand
Now, for the first time, I walk this path alone

I have traipsed along this trail a trillion times
So, how did I get so lost this time?

I took a stroll down our memory lane
The grass was unruly and unkept

Timeless

The bond that holds us
Timeless, boundless, merciless
Enduring cruel life

The In-Between

We either have every right in the world
Or not one single right at all

You either love me with all your heart
Or not even the smallest fragment

You either promise me forever
Or not a single second of time

I will know every inch of you—inside and out
Or else don't share a single memory or feeling

There can be no "in-between"
Not with what we're capable of being

Anything less than being "all in"
Is a desecration of our misplaced potential

I will no longer meet you in this in-between

Illusion or Delusion?

Abracadabra!
The red flags have all turned green
Elephants vanish

Tethered

My memories, all mangled
My devotion, betrayed
Our heartstrings are tangled
Still tethered, yet frayed

Planned with precision
Your words make me choke
Blinding my vision
With mirrors and smoke

Exploiting emotions
Manipulating time
I wrap up my notions
In some lies that rhyme

Suppressing defiance
To create a deflection
Feigning compliance
To escape this connection

Protégé

You aspire and assert
To be deeply adored
Turning the tide
From despised and abhorred

You craft and concoct
A perfect protégé
Out of popsicle sticks
And papiér mâché

You tinker and tweak
To get my temper just right
A dollop of dignity
A sprinkle of spite

You bedeck and bedazzle
With posh decoupage
Feeding me hummus
And pretentious fromage

You fidget and fret
As my façade starts to tarnish
So, you smear on some spackle
And two coats of varnish

You refine and refit
As I seem too ambitious
A miscalculation
Risks me turning auspicious

You juggle and jig
To conceal your delusion
As onlookers ponder
With concern and confusion

You dabble and dally
Correcting my blasphemy
Refusing to tolerate
Any contention or sass from me

You constrict and constrain
Fastening reins taught to me
Then adjust my demeanor
In a kitchen lobotomy

When this rouse gets too tricky
And I start to grow wise
You toss me out in the rain
Where I meet my demise

Heaven

I don't remember
The steps I took to heaven
But I know
I was there

At first,
I was there without you
But then, eventually
You caught up to me

Heaven was where
I learned to dance
In your arms
To our sappy songs

You drew a smile
Across my blank face
And promised
Never to erase it

It never rained
In our hallow heaven
Clouds softly adorned
Our powder-blue paradise

Heaven hadn't a bumpy road
Or a dead end
Just a straight path
Flourishing with flowers

I was always warm
In our happy heaven
Enclosed in your arms
In the soothing sun

But we weren't there alone

My demons followed me
As they always do
Crept right in
Through the crack in the door

My mindless mistake
Or subconscious slip-up
When I opened the door
To get some air

Our music
Suddenly stopped
Rain fell in sharp shards
Flooding the flowers

My smile was replaced
With a scathing scowl
You looked at me
With dismay and disgust

I was ripped from you
Bruised and bare
Led into a too-familiar
Dim, damp den

I tried to return to you
Unable to find the way
The roads twisted and turned
Into dead ends

A vicious voice
That sounded like my own
Whispered
"You don't belong here!"

In that moment
I awoke where I'm meant to be
Where I will always be
Far from heaven

I Am Too

I am too...
Carelessly available to you
When you correctly believe you need me
To rebuild and restore your aching ego
From your ruthless and relentless day

I am too...
Emotionally expressive to you
But only on your inconsistent terms
I wait for your actions to dictate my mood
Straining my tolerance for ambiguity

I am too...
Generous with giving my gifts to you
A consistent one-sided gift exchange
Sacrificing long-term peace and self-respect
For the momentary pleasure of this tit for tat

I am too...
Forgiving of your behavior
Washing away the blatant daily pain you cause
Pretending each new day restores me
I am the truest liar I know

I am too…

In love with you

Alone in this hopeless condition

Addicted to and enslaved by these feelings

I am too far gone to let you go

Forgiveness

Your words are wasps with switchblades
My deaf ear denies your ill intent
Forgiveness flows too freely

Just Say the Word

I've been biding my time
And waiting in vain
With my heart in a harness
And my sore bridled brain

I've constructed this fortress
Tiled each floor, papered each wall
Just say the word
And I'll demolish it all

My teetering emotions
Consoled in your eyes
I balance euphoria with anguish
Internally struggling to equalize

Worried "we" will blur into oblivion
When tortured by a moment
Then your voice, your scent, a memory
Shocks me back into atonement

Yet you alone possess
The rare remedy to fix this
Just say the word
For this misery's relentless

I'll wait for you in silence
A wary shadow while you mend
This painful path to follow
Would be worth it in the end

An authentic life to live
To lay our truths upon the table
Just say the word
And I'll defend you and enable

I declare my deep devotion
My entire soul, to you, I bestow
An audacious plea to choose me
Before I turn and let you go

With impending words unsaid
Boundless memories to create
Just say the word
And I will build our brilliant fate

Defenseless to our feelings
Our guilt we can absolve
Just say the word, my love
Let our fateful bond evolve

AUTUMN

Choose Me

You didn't choose me
The sentry of your secrets
Your warden of woes
The one who sees your true soul

You didn't choose me
The frisky little flirt
Your nit-witty wisecracker
The one who tickles your fancy

You didn't choose me
The pillar to your pride
Your forsaken, first fan
The one who spikes your spirit

You didn't choose me
The muse to your mushiness
Your winding wheel
The one who enlivens your luck

You didn't choose me
The Leia to your Han
Your dark-eyed kitten
The one who held your whole heart

You didn't choose me
You chose security, conformity, perception
An accustomed lifestyle, comfort...property
A long-lived lie

You didn't choose me
You chose deception—disguised as duty
Delaying life's inevitable love lessons
Denying examples of difficult decisions

So, with no other choice of my own...

I will choose me
Placing my sanity and self-respect
Above all false hope you ever fed me
Without ever defining what I was to you

I will choose me
To stave off the darkness that creeps in
Bound with the bitterness of rejection
Salvaging what is still left of my somber soul

I will choose me
Seeing myself as you mislead me to be
To give my deluded heart a fighting chance
For another man to cherish me...to choose me

Merciless Love

I placed my heart in your hands
Closing my eyes
You've since returned it to me
Mangled, yet wise

Missing you—on two occasions
Night and day
Merciless love
To make me feel this way

Holding onto my sanity
But not for long
Feeling six different emotions
When I hear our song

Mutilate my memory
So, I no longer reminisce
Harsh love
To make me ache like this

Blissful agony
Which choice to decry?
Living alone
Or living a lie?

One choice burns,
The other choice stings
Cruel love
To make me feel these things

A feeling between
Fury and sadness
Tender longing
With a touch of madness

Mementos of you
With every scent and sight
Vicious love
To scratch and bite

I'd face the harshest torture
To hold your hand once more
My precious love
The one I adore

I seek you everywhere
In reality, as well as dreams
Ruthless love
To rip open my seams

Once in a lifetime love
My "one"
My moon, my stars
My sun

Blindly placing within your hands,
My heart
Merciless love
To keep us apart

Dissolving Hope

Accustomed to torment
It's anguish I seek
My illusion implodes
With "I'll just take a peek"

A photo of you
A heart drawn in the sand
I watch hope dissolve
In the palm of my hand

Galas and ski trips
Your vacation collage
My "safe place" collapses
Now a perished mirage

Assumptions and assertions
Blurred the bold line
Between what's lucidly hers
And what's illusively mine

I've dwelled in delusion
In an ignorant abyss
Rewind time to twelve
When I lived blindly in bliss

Now compelled to accept
None of you belonged to me
With all of me bestowed to you
In an imagined reality

It's a Dream

At night
I hear you whisper
So clearly
Or so it would seem

But as I wake
My soul starts to ache
As I realize
It's just a dream

Monday Mourning

I still cry over you
Though only on Monday evenings
When I am all alone
For a single, somber hour

Balancing lavender and rose
In perfect measure
Reminiscent
Of our hotel baths

Sipping peppermint tea
The taste of our first kiss
Our tingly and tender lips
In my old decrepit kitchen

Taunting...haunting
Our playlist on shuffle
Some songs comfort me
While others wreck my soul

Flickering flames
Candles on the windowsill
Similar to the glare in your eyes
When you're half buzzed

Submerging into scorching memories
Sorrowful sentiments
Seeping out my pores
Trickling down with my tears

Pleading with me
Every single, sullen song
Urging me to wait for you
Or begging me to let you go

Nearing the hour's end
Wrinkled and raw
Tolerating torment
Until I hear that one, certain song

Lathering my body
With a lavender lotion
Painfully evocative
Of our post-shower massages

Clutching your t-shirt
Inhaling you into me
Choking on your essence
Inviting in your presence

Staring longingly, and desperately
Into the murky mirror
Materializing your mirage
Standing behind me

Adorning your t-shirt
Buried in my benevolent bed
Mesmerizing my mind
To meet you in our in-between

Waking abruptly
On Tuesday morning
Listlessly stripping
My sorrow-scented sheets

Traipsing half-consciously
Into the awaking shower
Monday mourning
Swirls down the drain

Applying my mask
Cloaked in an ill-fitted costume
I head out into the week ahead
Until Monday comes again

The Next "The One"

In aching despair
Searching for the next "the one"
Red flags at half mast

The Emptiness

The heaviest weight I carry
Is the emptiness inside of me
In the space you once occupied
So fully and effectively

I would have thought
That the absence of your smirky smile
Adoring gaze, and tender touch
Would make me lighter...

But longing weighs ten tons

Your Key in the Door

In my sorrow I seek
Your blue shirt in my drawer
Your chipped mug in the sink
Your wet towel on the floor

In my sorrow I seek
The watch that you wore
The scent of your hair
That smile I adore

In my sorrow I seek
The pulse of your snore
The shift in your step
Your key in the door

The absence of these
Too overt to ignore
This sorrow I seek
Too dire to endure

In Pieces

I try to reconstruct you
To recreate your signature scent
Reliving all that we have been through
Revisiting places where we went

You come back to me in pieces
With the pungent pines in the park
In the subtle scent of "new car" leather
And in smoky wafts after dark

A long whiff of a fresh Corona
Mixed with a breeze of salty sea
If I close my eyes tightly
That brings you back to me

I've sampled every lotion
Tested every single spray
I cannot find you in a bottle
So, I cannot make you stay

Your Letters

I came across your letters today

My wrists ached from the weight of the paper
My eyes were blinded by the scribbled ink
Your voice in my ears roared into white noise
And the void in my chest grew into a chasm

Will your letters ever be just "letters?"

The End of Our Song

At first glance
The mind ignores
Golden knobs
On splintered doors

Cracks along
The yellow brick road
What the mirror
Truly showed

Quiet souls
In noisy bars
Broken hearts
On subway cars

Porcelain angels
With chipped-up wings
Men who hide
Their wedding rings

A worthwhile wait
On a line too long
The flutter felt
When they play our song

At first glance
The mind perceives
From where he comes
And the way he leaves

Scars that stain
A pretty face
The one who didn't
Win the race

A tighter fit
From extra pounds
The way a lover's
Snoring sounds

The red ink scrawled
Across works of art
The idle ache
When we're apart

The hollow hell
Of a night too long
My aching heart
At the end of our song

Eviscerated

You know—you have always known me
You have known this all along
You've recognized my amorous stare
My tingly touch and the scent of my hair

I tried so hard to reach you sooner
But I got lost along the way
The mockingbirds played tricks on me
The fog was thick and I could not see

I set you securely in my visions
Every detail planned and plotted
The fortune teller foretold our fate
Yet the universe conspired to wait

Despite our apparent bond
You feebly fought against it
My weary words scantily touched you
My bare admissions barely broke through

You see, I've eviscerated myself
Emptied out all that I am, all I ever would be
With the hope that you would remember
In all this mess—the faintest burning ember

And now, with all my insides and outsides
Splattered on the sand before me
I wait, immobile, for the tide to come astray
To eliminate the wasted mess—drag it all away

When we return, again, with our wiser souls
I vow to be more convincing
You will realize I'm your soul to cherish
Not disembowel to watch me perish

Holding On

Holding on
With all the will I possess
Not loosening my grip
Not letting go

Holding on,
I shut my eyes
I feel pain, yet I persist
Not letting go

Holding on
I feel myself weaken
I cry away my fear
Not letting go

Holding on
My heart and mind ache
I stay conscious as my blood drains
Not letting go

Holding on
I lose the beat of my heart
I feel you slip away from me
Not letting go

Holding on
As you leave my arms
I'm as cold as stone
Letting go

Us

You said, *"let's be 'us' again"*
For just one night
We were both aching for it
Brutally building up to it
Since we reunited

Without hesitation
I gave in—knowing it would end me
And that for you
It would merely be nostalgic
You have that talent of suppressing emotions

Despite how often
You would cruelly pull away from me
Then relentlessly return again
I hoped this might make you stay
Consistently and endlessly

So, while we were being "us"
I buried what was left of me
Somewhere dark and impenetrable
Never to return again
Never to be part of an "us"

Nostalgia

We both know
All too well
That not all sad songs
Are temperate love ballads

Some have a rapid rhythm
And a brisk beat
Triggering nostalgia
Of our languishing love

Ripping out our guts
Frantically flinging them
Against an alabaster wall
Splattering and spilling into art

Far too hideous
To endure facing—and yet
Far too captivating
To ever look away

Bait and Switch

I wrote you a song
It sits in silence—it sits unsung
Tripping on
My timid tongue

Avoiding my gaze
Evading my grips
With one foot out the door
And an excuse on your lips

It sounds like sincerity
But lies have a scent
Your words were most fragrant
The deeper we went

The red flags flailing
The elephant in the room
Shoved into the closet
Where my skeletons loom

With my deaf ear and blind eye
I hear and see your mirage
In defiant denial
A secret sabotage

Enticed and mislead
A neatly woven "bait and switch"
With flecks of gold and silver
In every stealthy stitch

The Buffet

Snatching up a sizable slice
And a full scoop
Carving off far more
Than you could ever consume

Flagrantly filling your flute
Until it overflows
Gulping and guzzling
Without any regard

Hastily heaping
A second hefty helping
Gobbling and gorging
In full-on gluttony

Double dipping
Disregarding all decency
Slovenly slobbering
And sloppily spitting

Poking your pompous pinky
Into the pudding
Fondling the confections
With your fleshy fingers

Nibbling and gnawing
Off the tastiest tidbits
Unappreciative
Of the full, divine delicacy

Rapaciously pocketing
Some treats for later
Just in case
You have a late-night a craving

Coveting the last
Cut of the cake
Greedily denying others
Of any delight

Picking at your plate
Repugnantly playing
Making a mangled mess
Only to discard it

Casually covering up
Your wanton waste
When conscious
Of your carelessness

Tossing away
Your tormented trash
As you head back to the buffet
For another helping

Angel

A kink in my past
With throes, I do tell
An angel in black
Whom had fallen from hell

Common and cold
These souls of clone
He laughed in his heart
As my trust had grown

Luring me
From the drowning sea
He awaited my praise
But received my plea

A winsome face
In which two shadows show
The first, of friend
The other, of foe

Conspiring to
Escape my grip
He sent a potion
For my lips to sip

Acute in my senses
I feared my fate
Smelling the poison
Of his liquefied hate

Dead was my love
For the angel in black
Who traded my heart
And stabbed my turned back

Poisonous Bite

A horrid cry
To which none respond
Broken by air
Eternally gone

Said but once
Not to repeat
Clenched by clouds
Dissolved in heat

A last resort
To save from death
All life escapes
In torn-out breath

Barren of others
The land grew tight
Shocking death
By a poisonous bite

Shame

My outcast arms
Now lie lame
Holding my head
That fell in shame

Monster

I tiptoed around
Your fragile ego
Silently screaming
To let me go

You maimed my mind
Like a mad mosquito
Forbidding my freedom
With a violent veto

You labeled me
"lazy"
Then,
"Bat-shit crazy"

Your hateful head
All hot and hazy
Clenching your teeth
With your eyes all glazy

I bore the blame
For your mistakes
To avoid the rage
Your wrath creates

You're a puppeteer
Who manipulates
A narcissist
Who hurts and hates

With your small mind
And tiny hands
Making large waves
And mountains grand

I've endured more dread
Than I could withstand
You gaslighting monster
And your cruel command

Jealousy

Blindly blazing
In your charms
Attain the soul
That none alarms

Jealousy
Now cast and formed
My silence screams
Scathing and scorned

No glory glimmers
In my envious eyes
Just raging revenge
For whom I despise

Marveling in
Your mystic merit
Repelled remorse
You now inherit

My sect of serpents
For you, I'll unfurl
Burn in their bitter
And fear them uncurl

Forging your lies
That fools believe
You pilfered my pride
Which I rightly retrieve

My eminent envy
I sorely restrain
Instead, I ingest it
And pray in pain

For in the end
I'll thank the fates
As you hang in the hell
That my craze creates

Traitor

Is that your face
Beneath the shade?
Crawling through
The mess you've made?

I durably deny
I know of you
The friends you've kept
Are foolish and few

How dare you tell
Of all your tales
As you feast upon
Your meal of snails

Alone you sit
All drunk with drinks
Strangling your neck
With fluffy minks

The trip you took
Wasn't worth the ride
Now here you are
Without your pride

Fatty cat
Who pays for pats
Is that you
Sleeping with the rats?

You took and take
All prior to thought
Don't you know
How friends are bought?

Silly snake
Crawl out from the dirt
No one left
For you to hurt?

You should have known
You were to lose
I'd hate to be standing
In your stolen shoes

Peaceful Stranger

Shot into
A scene of dark
Triggered by
A violent spark

Stolen from the lungs
All breath
Falling into
A silent death

You think you're in
A lonely night
But soon engulf
Yourself in fright

Perceiving all
Your ground erase
Vanished pain
While keeping pace

Feeling all
But not with senses
Grip your soul
As peace commences

Into light
Your vision is cast
Arousing sights
Of filtered past

No one there
Yet not alone
Emerging through
The light that shone

Touch the hand
Of the peaceful stranger
A looming warmth
A lapse of danger

Enveloped in
His holy womb
Your soul in peace
Your corpse—a tomb

Left the world
Of all existence
Enter death
With no resistance

The Bargaining Stage

Apparently,
I have entered the "bargaining" stage
Along my grief journey
Whatever that even means

Does bargaining require haggling?
With nothing left to barter
I have agreed to the terms
I am contritely complying

Bargaining feels like
Holding on to hollow hope
Searching fervently for covert clues
Reconstructing reality

Foolishly and desperately
I may linger here too long—or forever
Refusing acceptance
Denying our demise

Drift Away

The weight I carried
No longer on my shoulders
I may drift away

Alone

I have lost my identity
Or so it seems
Full of fickle wishes
And falsified dreams

Clear and soundless
Not quite whole
No inner voice
Void of a soul

I've disappeared
Not touched by light
Not sought out nor cared for
Emanating fright

Nomadic and loveless
With unheard breath
I'll continue alone
Until caught by death

The Reality

The reality is
None of this was ever really "real"
An invention of my loneliness
And your boredom

Doting words, flirtatious glances
And tender gestures
Merely deceptive sounds
And misleading motions

Mementos and tokens
Tucked into your pockets
Just twisted trophies
Of your trysts and triumphs

Our discreet meetings
And backdoor deals
An adrenaline rush
Your revenge for feeling neglected

I was never truly
The *"prettiest girl in the world"*
Or the *"most perfect person"*
As you spewed to me—was I?

The 1400 photos…85 songs
Cautiously curated
Surely, far less
Than what you've pinned to her shrine

You once claimed
To love me with your whole heart
Perhaps you have multiple hearts
Like a squid

The reality is
None of this was ever really "real"
An invention of my loneliness
And your boredom

Deceive

An effect like drowning
Has come over me
With fear and frowning
At what will never be

Lies torn and told
By tongues that lie
In my heart, I behold
And alone, I cry

To recall my goodness
Would now be a sin
For my misery shadows it
All my goodness—forgotten

I am evil and twisted
Or so you believe
Your notions mislead you
Our memories, you deceive

The feelings I claimed
You have stolen and burned
The hatred you sent me
I now have returned

Worthy

Resolved with resent
I'm not your design
Yet search your own soul
Is it worthy of mine?

WINTER

Yesterday

Stealing back
My yesterday
Now burnt to ashes
Blown away

Abducted by
Relentless today
Lost with sleep
In dark now lay

My soul remained
My body forbade
For only in dreams
I could have stayed

So, as night darkens
And daydreams fade
A goodnight kiss
I knelt and prayed

Boiled into
A memory stew
Consumed by my soul
For my mind to chew

Extinguished in
The breeze that blew
Rekindled in
A déjà vu

Enveloped in
A November day
Stolen from
The arms of May

Chameleon days
All blend to gray
Raping
Yellow yesterday

Drowning deep
In time's great lake
I grasp it with
My hands that shake

Holding tight
For all my sake
Though in its death
Today will wake

Cruel Time

Father Time
Has either an exceptional sense of humor
Or else, he is a sadistic prick

Either way,
He is entertained by watching us fools
While eating a large bucket of popcorn

I hope he chokes on a kernel

The Fool

Beware of the fool
Once she unravels the joke
Jesters reign harshly

Lament

On an ordinary mundane day
A certain song, a familiar scent
Will ignite a blaze in your calloused core
And you'll start the steps to true lament

Aching for my amorous arms
Longing for my consoling voice
You'll resent the ill and effortless effect
Of your irreversible, forever choice

Despite your personal promise
You will feel compelled to seek me
Searching my name fuels instant regret
Intrigued by a photo you can't unsee

Overlooking a landscape—familiar, yet old
My back to the camera, appearing alone
Admiring twilight, wine in my hand
My expression obscure, emotions unknown

What feelings am I feeling
As I stare across the sky?
Did I bring you with me?
Is your heartbeat still nearby?

Searching more, digging deeper
With fast and feverish fingers
To uncover my mysterious mood
To find if any of you still lingers

Suddenly, the company you keep
The "Side B" songs of an obscure band
The tapenade and top-shelf whisky
All white noise, and blatantly bland

Compelled to find a sensible reason
An extenuating circumstance
You draft and redraft a simple message
Lacking the courage to take that chance

Feeling a merciless and tender longing
As you pace the rooms of your empty home
You'll realize what I tried to convey
Through every word in every poem

My Silence

Your words are weapons
Wounding me, yet unaware
My sly silence slays

Disillusion

The moonlight drew out
Shapeless shadows
Stealing the life
From the evening primrose

Disillusion crept in
And threatened to stay
I hid in the shadows
And prayed for the day

A familiar whisper
That boomed like a shout
Said *"Come out of the shadows"*
"Ride this one out!"

Taking some steps
While watching my feet
My pace then quickened
I felt my heartbeat

With my thoughts assured
My woe restrained
Hope emerged
And the moonlight waned

Then the ascending sun
In its crimson glory
Washed the day
Of all its worry

Crumbs

Sprinkling crumbs of hope
With *"maybe someday"*
Keeping me on a string
With *"I miss you"*

In time
My appetite grew too grand
To live on your
Meatless morsels

The string
From which you strung me
Frayed and worn
Began to strangle me

In time
I compelled myself
To satisfy my appetite
And found I was no longer hungry

So, I cut the string
That tethered me to you
And tied it into a bow
Affixing it upon my gift of freedom

I Dissent

If my whistle doesn't blow
And my wheels don't squeak
They will label me "passive"
They will say I'm "too meek"

So, with ardent conviction
These decrees, I dissent
Your rules—they oppress
Your norms—they prevent

I've uncensored my silence
Soothed my once-bitten lip
As I candidly convey
My own valiant script

Mirror

How dare you judge me
Without wearing my scarred skin
Did your mirror break?

Your Happiness

Wherever I look
On every page
On every site
Your success and your happiness
Flashes and flaunts before me

Yet I wonder…
Why you are not present in those moments
Looking into your loved ones' eyes
Instead of looking at them
Through the lens of your camera

Awaking Hope

A nameless emotion
Alike to fear
Had overcome and infested
Our atmosphere

Tyranny through trickery
We were mislead
Our values—refurbished
Our conscience—retread

Bonds of faithful family
And fondest friends
Ripped and ruined
Without amends

Then you appeared
With infectious fervor
A lantern in darkness
A life preserver

Conviction with kindness
Constructing trust
Directly denouncing
The vile and unjust

Astonishingly wise
Beyond your years
An assuring voice
To annul our fears

Insisting integrity
Versus treason
Hailing humanity
Verses unreason

Staying your course
And waging your word
Bonds are rebuilding
Your voice is now heard

Awaking hope
In hollowed hearts
Uniting the lost
As your promise imparts

Survival Skills

Fleeing floods
And hiking hills
I'll show you
My survival skills

Scratching and scraping
To scale the wall
Through knife-like vines
I creep and crawl

Who else could build
This nest of nails
Then furnish it
With nightingales?

Weeding out
Every snake and louse
Pardon me
I'm "the man of the house"

Binding burdens
That drown and drag
I carry this weight
In a Chanel bag

Blocked and blinded
From words that scour
Tormenting tongues
Ignite my power

By day I wear
My "Kate" costumes
As twilight nears
Catherine resumes

Want to learn how
I win my wills?
I'll show you
My survival skills

Home Improvements

I've made some home improvements

Wrapped my fence in barbed wire
Erected a steel gate
Adorned my den with daggers
Bred bobcats in my basement
And planted pythons in the garden

Enter at your own risk

Accessories

We all have demons
Mine wear nice accessories
And use good grammar

The Recipe

The recipe for moving on is quite simple
And the ingredients are plentiful

Ingredients:
4 heaping cups of disappointment
3 cups of frustration
2 tablespoons of anger
1 teaspoon of confusion
1 pinch of disdain
1 dash of jealousy
1 sprinkle of false hope

Instructions:
Pour all ingredients into a large pot
Set it on high heat
Stir vigorously until the clumps dissolve

Bring it to a rapid boil
Cover it with a lid when it gets too vigorous
Remove from heat
Let it cool (while you seek out a new lover)

Top it with self-respect
Garnish it with hope

Buried

I am finally ready to remember you
Yet I have buried you
Somewhere so dark and far away
And burned the map to ashes

The Last Poem

They say that I will officially be "over" you
When you no longer inspire my poems

I will return to writing about the sea, the sun
Or the mundane details of the seasons

This longing has dragged on far too long
And you have cluttered far too many pages

I am taking matters into my own, shaky hands
This is the last poem I will ever write for you

The last time I cry over my tattered notebook
Scribbling words that rhyme with "yearning"

The last time I search synonyms for "pain"
Or try to fit my anguish into six syllables

No more researching shades of green
Or qualities of light to describe your eyes

I'll end the quest for the perfect, elusive word
To describe the thrill I feel when we touch

You have inspired my most authentic work
By activating all my volatile, inner voices

My pen, pressed to paper, is drained of hope
It scantily leaves a mark anymore

So, I will burn the map to our memory lane
And sprinkle all the ashes onto these pages

I'll silence the songs that play out our folktale
And in time, refurbish them as new memories

I'll stop straddling a line between holding on
And ultimately, helplessly, letting you go

Although my visceral verses are not in vain
They are powerless against our futile affection

I am taking matters into my own, shaky hands
This is the last poem I will ever write for you

Opening Our Eyes

Have we neared the end of our dream?

As we wake, we might open our eyes
To doubt in the doorway
Failure in our faces
Or solitude a step away

Instead, we may wake to discover
Independence
A sense of direction
Or means to security

We will have to open our eyes to see

Perhaps we would rather
Linger in our past
Secure in each other's arms
Planning our futures together

Not anticipating true reality
Pulling each other through emotions
Never imagining this day
When we would have to cry alone

Together, we matured
We fell in love—and had our hearts broken
Together, we met victory
And felt defeat

Together, we must use our past
To create our own future
Together, we are here today in the present,
Afraid to open our eyes

Yes—we have neared the end of our dream
But as we wake,
We will open our eyes to our future
Where alone, we will learn to dream again

I Am

I am what you think
Bold, or meek; clever, or dull
I'm insidious

No Inward Search

A tangy smile
That hides her jest
Merry eyes
That plague with zest

Peering through
Her ignorant mind
No inward search
In fear of what she'd find

All her pain
In a laugh she envelopes
Twisting her heart
As despair develops

In a glance
Her glee you'll see
Stare too long
Pure misery

Resisting her truth
For all her sake
But in due time
Her soul will break

Elusive

Deftly disassembling
The traits that make me whole
A yellow extrovert shell
Shields my green introvert soul

No one truly knows me
And that is by design
Protecting frail emotions
Yours, as well as mine

At times I've sprinkled crumbs
Bits and fragments of the true me
After my second glass of Cabernet
Or during twilight by the sea

I am a living contradiction
And as time goes on, I learn
The more I stay elusive
The less I will return

My Flaws

I am flawed in places…
Places you will never see…
See them and you may leave…
Leave with my heart in your hands…
Hands that can destroy…
Destroy our dear memories…
Memories where my flaws were "quirks"

Before…

Before you saw them as flaws…
Flaws that you can't unsee…
Unsee what you've seen so you could feel…
Feel what you felt when you didn't look…
Look for my flaws…
Flaws that define me

Misunderstood

Amber strands
Fall out of place
The framework of
A modest face
Cast alone
She finds her space

Alone in pain
Alone insane

Never mind
Her words that scour
Her thoughts start sweet
But then turn sour
Her smile
Like water to a wilting flower

Ever meet her?
Perhaps you should
You'd see her wit
Her charm, her good
Instead, she's left
Misunderstood

My Inspiration

"Your poems are dark!"
(He only likes limericks)
Anguish inspires me

Perpetual Seasons

A pallor cast
Upon the ground
Observing winds
Of tranquil sound

Like the dream
I dreamt last night
The amber colored trees
Fade white

Dew drops drip
Off morning glories
Birds sings songs
To narrate stories

Yellow now
Overcomes blue air
Reflecting off water
A gallant glare

Chameleon character
Of falling leaves
Wind returns
As skin perceives

Cooler days
Early nights
All dried the fields
Grey tints our sights

My Golden Girls

I once was weary
In a shambled shell
For no one else
Had known me well

In equal exchange
Of fears and feelings
I felt unsheltered
My shell, you were stealing

Consigning secrets
And trending true
My trust I gave
Your trust then grew

Maddening moments
Frivolous fights and furies
All long since forgiven
Now "remember when" stories

Stubborn stances
With barely a budge
Somehow surrendered
With never a grudge

Hardships have happened
We'll brace for some more
Ever in devotion
Our bond will endure

The Rose to my Dorothy
And for countless more years
We'll eat cheesecake in robes
And laugh through our tears

My Ancient Soul

So, near the end
When my fate will unfold
And my story
Is ready to be told

You'll know the angst
Of my ancient soul
That sought out sorrow
And felt it all

My Debts to Karma

They echo *"you deserve better"*
Unaware of these secrets I keep
Karma's reckless debtor
Liabilities grow steep

"How dare anyone hurt you?"
My "goodness" they all see
I'm aware of each cardinal virtue
Obeying only three

I weave my peculiar pattern
My subconscious stroll to relapse
My transgressions barely matter
I'm inculpable, perhaps

Yet my guilt does overwhelm me
And in my poetry, I repent
Under the limbs of an old elm tree
I record what I've overspent

I will repay my debts to karma
Then fixate on the receipt
My enslavement to the drama
Will cause my credit line to repeat

About the Author

I've always had a fascination with vocabulary. I recall stringing words together as young as age four, making up nursery rhymes and recreating song lyrics to amuse others.

Starting around age six, my aunt Eleanor would read words to me from a dictionary and quiz me on their meanings. I soon graduated to reading thesauruses—which is when I began developing my knack for wordsmithing— conveying my thoughts in alternate words that rhymed or alliterated.

Despite these introverted interests, I am perceived to be an extrovert, as I enjoy entertaining others and thrive on (positive) attention. So, as an extroverted introvert, I have put myself into high-emotion situations, only to then recoil and reflect on these experiences—recording the details in tattered notebooks.

This book is a compilation of over half a lifetime of emotions—telling the story of who I was, who I am, and how I have evolved—and continue to evolve. Although my profile might be that of a typical professional, middle-aged, single mother of two sons living in the northeast United States, who I truly am is conveyed on these pages. I have weaved together poems written at age 12, age 46, and every age in-between. Although my specific experiences have been vastly different across this timespan, the emotions are the same.

I have organized this collection by the four seasons, reflecting how emotions—like seasons—follow a perpetual cycle, with blurred beginnings and endings, yet sharp distinctions. I start with Spring, representing the hopefulness and bliss of a new love, and traverse through uncertainty (Summer), heartbreak (Autumn), and self-healing (Winter).

Despite the recurring nature of the seasons, I tend to dwell in Autumn, where I feel most at home, therefore, Eternal Autumn seemed to be the most fitting title for this collection.

About the Publisher

Glass Spider Publishing was founded in 2016 by writer Vince Font to help independent and self-published authors reach readers through professionally edited and artfully designed books. The company is headquartered in Ogden, Utah, but has published authors throughout the world including the United States, Canada, England, Kenya, South Korea, and Vietnam.

GLASS
SPIDER
PUBLISHING

www.glassspiderpublishing.com

CPSIA information can be obtained
at www.ICGtesting.com
Printed in the USA
BVHW091817021222
653303BV00006B/572